For my sister, April,
who feeds minds every day.

– Lisl H. Detlefsen

For the farmers who work
so hard to feed us all. Thank you!
– Renée Kurilla

Text copyright © 2019 by Lisl H. Detlefsen
Illustrations copyright © 2019 by Renee Kurilla

ISBN 978-1-948898-00-3

Library of Congress Control Number: 2018956937

Published by FEEDING MINDS PRESS, Washington, D.C.
Book design by Mary A. Burns   Edited by Emma D. Dryden

Printed in the United States of America
10 9 8 7 6 5 4 3

Right This Very Minute

a table-to-farm book about food and farming

by Lisl H. Detlefsen   illustrated by Renée Kurilla

FEEDING MINDS PRESS

American Farm Bureau Foundation for Agriculture®

What's that you say?
You're hungry for breakfast?

Right this very minute?

Then you need a farmer.

You have the stories of so many,
right here on your table.

Right this very minute in a citrus grove, a grower tests oranges for ripeness.

When the fruit is ready, the harvesting crew will pick the oranges, which will be squeezed into the juice you drink in the morning.

Right this very minute in a new field on a wheat farm, a farmer drills furrows the perfect depth for seeds.

Your pancakes were made with wheat that was grown, harvested, and then ground into flour.

Right this very minute in a sugarbush
filled with maple trees, a sugarmaker
replaces old collection buckets with a
new tubing system to carry maple sap
to a storage tank.

The sap will be boiled down in evaporators until it becomes thick and sweet like the maple syrup you've poured on your pancakes.

What's that you say?
You'd like a snack?

Right this very minute?

Then you need a farmer.

You have the knowledge of so many, right here in your hands.

Right this very minute, as the sun sets on a cranberry marsh, a grower starts protecting the crop from frost.

The grower will be up all night checking the sprinklers that keep the plants from freezing, all so cranberries can become part of your trail mix.

Right this very minute, on a southern farm, a peanut farmer installs soil sensors to make sure the fields aren't too wet or too dry.

The sensors help the farmer decide when and how much to water these sensitive plants.

What's that you say?
It's time for lunch?

Right this very minute?

Then you need a farmer.

You have the hard work of so many,
right here in your lunchbox.

Right this very minute, a dairy farmer tends the cows.

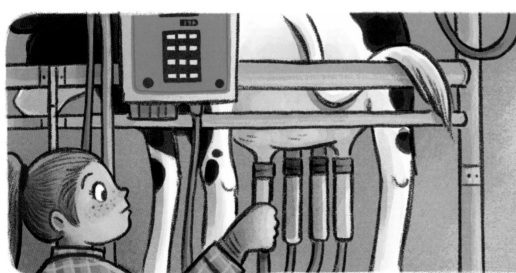

The cheese in your sandwich was made with milk from cows that must be milked at least twice every day, whether it's a weekday, a Saturday, a birthday, or a holiday.

Right this very minute, farmers till and test the soil for nutrients to make sure it's healthy before planting seeds that will grow into long, crunchy carrots.

Right this very minute, an apple grower works with a beekeeper to bring beehives into an orchard.

Hundreds of thousands of honeybees will pollinate the pale pink blossoms, helping each tree grow many bushels of apples for you to enjoy.

What's that you say?
You're ready for dinner?

Right this very minute?

Then you need a farmer.

You have the pride of so many,
right here on your plate.

Right this very minute, a cattle rancher moves the herd to a wide pasture to graze. She cares for the cows and welcomes their calves into the world.

When the calves are old enough, they will move to new pastures or feedyards before they are harvested for the beef that will be made into hamburgers.

Right this very minute, a farmer plans a crop rotation schedule to keep the soil healthy and grow more of the very best vegetables, like the potato you've topped with broccoli and cheese.

Right this very minute, some farmers prepare produce for delivery to grocery stores and others box it up to sell at local farmer's markets.

Before lettuce and tomatoes ever get tossed in a salad or put on top of a hamburger, they must travel from the farm to hungry customers.

What's that you say?
You'd like dessert?

Right this very minute?

Then you need a farmer and,
sometimes, a whole farming family.

You have the dedication of so many,
right here on your fork.

Right this very minute, a grower checks the weather forecast in a family-owned strawberry patch while workers help hundreds of visitors pick their own strawberries.

Right this very minute, a family checks their backyard coop to make sure the chickens have enough feed and fresh water.

Then they collect eggs that get made into foods like the shortcake in your bowl.

What's that you say?
You want to grow your own food?

Right this very minute?

Then you need to think like a farmer.

You can help plant a garden
right here in your community.

Right this very minute, you and your friends, family, and neighbors can work together to choose which crops to grow in your gardens.

In a few months, you will enjoy healthy snacks and meals made with the fruits and vegetables you harvest yourselves.

Every single day of every year, farmers tend their crops, care for their animals, and work hard to feed their families and yours.

Next time you eat your breakfast, snack, lunch, dinner, or dessert, remember that somewhere, right this very minute, there's a farmer to thank for your delicious food.

And if some day you decide to become a farmer, right that very minute you'll be doing your part to feed the world, too.

For **free educational activities** and videos from **REAL** farmers showing what they are up to **right this very minute!**

visit: www.feedingmindspress.org

The goal of **FEEDING MINDS PRESS** is to create and publish **accurate** and **engaging books** about **agriculture.**

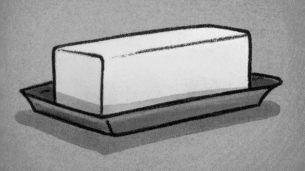